love from Great Aunt Kerrie
2024

Published in 2006 by Simply Read Books
www.simplyreadbooks.com

Copyright © 2006 by Duncan Weller
www.duncanweller.com

Cataloguing in Publication Data

Weller, Duncan, 1965–
The boy from the sun / Duncan Weller.
ISBN -10: 1–894965–33–7
ISBN -13: 978–1–894965–33–0
1. Nature —Juvenile fiction. I. Title.
PS8645.E45B69 2006   jC813'.6   C2006-900016-6

Book design by Doug McCaffry

Color separations by Scanlab

10 9 8 7 6 5 4 3 2 1

Printed in Italy

We gratefully acknowledge the support of the Canada Council for the Arts for our publishing program.

The Boy from the Sun

Duncan Weller

by Duncan Weller

On a cold grey
nothing sort of day
halfway
between home and school
sat three sad children.

They said nothing,
and could only stare.

Out of the sky
came a little body...

...with a big yellow shining head.

He landed on the concrete sidewalk
next to the three sad children.

"Why are you so sad?" he asked.

The children said nothing.
They could only stare.

"I will show you something,"
said the boy from the sun.

"Keep your eyes open!"

And out from nothing
came a beautiful bird
with magnificent wings.

"Oh!" cheered the children.
"It's magic!"

"I will show you more,"
said the boy from the sun.

"Follow me."

The concrete sidewalk broke.

The children ran into the field to play.

"I have a poem for you," said the boy
   from the sun.

"I see and hear and feel the breeze today,
   And all the paths of leaves are in the air,
   Yet on a sidewalk you sit and stare,
   Wishing you were somewhere far away.
   But through all great minds
   And through all great art
   Many paths are laid
   When first beats your brave heart.

   For here, with everyone,
   You are splinters of the sun,
   You are worth celebrating,
   You are worth elevating,
   And when you take the time
   To fill your worlds within
   You will join the world without.

Then Chance and Choice and Change
Will spring like grass
And fly beyond the trees
Where you will have all the paths of leaves,
As in the air."

The three happy children clapped,
and the boy with the shining yellow head
flew back up in to the sky
toward the sun.